KING GRISLY-BEARD

A Tale from the Brothers Grimm

WANTED!
EXTRAORDINARY
ACTOR & ACTRESS
TO PLAY THE
LEADING ROLES
IN WILHELM &
JACOB GRIMM'S
FABULOUS
KING GRISLY-BEARD
INQUIRE WITHIN →

GRR!

IMPRESARIO

KING GRISLY-BEARD

Translated by Edgar Taylor

Pictures by MAURICE SENDAK

A Sunburst Book

Michael di Capua Books

Farrar, Straus and Giroux

The Edgar Taylor translation of *King Grisly-Beard*
was originally published in 1823 in *German Popular Tales*,
the first English edition of tales from Grimm.

For Sheila Weinberg
M.S.

A great king had a daughter who was very beautiful, but so proud and haughty and conceited that none of the princes who came to ask her in marriage were good enough for her, and she only made sport of them.

Once upon a time the king held a great feast, and invited all her suitors; and they sat in a row according to their rank, kings and princes and dukes and earls. Then the princess came in and passed by them all, but she had something spiteful to say to every one. The first was too fat: "He's as round as a tub," said she.

The next was too tall: "What a maypole!" said she.
The next was too short: "What a dumpling!" said she.
The fourth was too pale, and she called him "Wallface."
The fifth was too red, so she called him "Cockscomb."
The sixth was not straight enough, so she said he was
like a green stick that had been laid to dry over a baker's

oven. And thus she had some joke to crack upon every one.

But she laughed more than all at a good king who was there. "Look at him," said she, "his beard is like an old mop, he shall be called Grisly-Beard." So the king got the nickname of Grisly-Beard.

But the old king was very angry when he saw how his daughter behaved, and how she ill-treated all his guests; and he vowed that, willing or unwilling, she should marry the first beggar that came to the door.

Two days after there came by a travelling musician, who began to sing under the window, and beg alms: and when the king heard him, he said, "Let him come in." So they brought in a dirty-looking fellow; and when he had sung before the king and the princess, he begged a

boon. Then the king said, "You have sung so well that I will give you my daughter for your wife." The princess begged and prayed; but the king said, "I have sworn to give you to the first beggar, and I will keep my word." So words and tears were of no avail; the parson was sent for, and she was married to the musician.

When this was over, the king said, "Now get ready to go; you must not stay here; you must travel on with your husband."

Then the beggar departed, and took her with him; and they soon came to a great wood. "Pray," said she, "whose is this wood?" "It belongs to King Grisly-Beard," answered he; "hadst thou taken him, all had been thine." "Ah! unlucky wretch that I am!" sighed she, "would that I had married King Grisly-Beard!" Next they came to some fine meadows. "Whose are these beautiful green meadows?" said she. "They belong to King Grisly-Beard; hadst thou taken him, they had all been thine." "Ah! unlucky wretch that I am!" said she, "would that I had married King Grisly-Beard!"

Then they came to a great city. "Whose is this noble city?" said she. "It belongs to King Grisly-Beard; hadst thou taken him, it had all been thine." "Ah! miserable wretch that I am!" sighed she, "why did I not marry King Grisly-Beard?" "That is no business of mine," said the musician; "why should you wish for another husband? am not I good enough for you?"

At last they came to a small cottage. "What a paltry place!" said she; "to whom does that little dirty hole belong?" The musician answered, "That is your and my house, where we are to live."

"Where are your servants?" cried she. "What do we want with servants?" said he, "you must do for yourself whatever is to be done. Now make the fire, and put on water and cook my supper, for I am very tired." But the princess knew nothing of making fires and cooking, and the beggar was forced to help her. When they had eaten a very scanty meal they went to bed; but the musician called her up very early in the morning to clean the house. Thus they lived for two days: and when they had eaten up all there was in the cottage, the man said, "Wife, we can't go on thus, spending money and earning nothing. You must learn to weave baskets." Then he

went out and cut willows and brought them home, and she began to weave; but it made her fingers very sore. "I see this work won't do," said he, "try and spin; perhaps you will do that better." So she sat down and tried to spin; but the threads cut her tender fingers till the blood ran. "See now," said the musician, "you are good for nothing, you can do no work;—what a bargain I have got! However, I'll try and set up a trade in pots and pans, and you shall stand in the market and sell them." "Alas!" sighed she, "when I stand in the market and any of my father's court pass by and see me there, how they will laugh at me!"

But the beggar did not care for that; and said she must work, if she did not wish to die of hunger. At first the trade went well; for many people, seeing such a beautiful woman, went to buy her wares, and paid their money without thinking of taking away the goods. They lived on this as long as it lasted, and then her husband bought a fresh lot of ware, and she sat herself down with it in the corner of the market; but a drunken soldier soon came by, and rode his horse against her stall and broke all her goods into a thousand pieces. Then she began to weep, and knew not what to do. "Ah! what will become of me!" said she; "what will my husband say?" So she

ran home and told him all. "Who would have thought you would have been so silly," said he, "as to put an earthernware stall in the corner of the market, where everybody passes?—But let us have no more crying; I see you are not fit for this sort of work: so I have been to the king's palace, and asked if they did not want a kitchen-maid, and they have promised to take you, and there you will have plenty to eat."

Thus the princess became a kitchen-maid, and helped the cook to do all the dirtiest work: she was allowed to carry home some of the meat that was left, and on this she and her husband lived.

She had not been there long before she heard that the king's eldest son was passing by, going to be married; and she went to one of the windows and looked out. Everything was ready, and all the pomp and splendour of the court was there. Then she thought with an aching heart on her own sad fate, and bitterly grieved for the pride and folly which had brought her so low. And the servants gave her some of the rich meats, which she put into her basket to take home.

All on a sudden, as she was going out, in came the king's son in golden clothes: and when he saw a beautiful woman at the door, he took her by the hand, and said she should be his partner in the dance: but she trembled

for fear, for she saw that it was King Grisly-Beard, who was making sport of her. However, he kept fast hold and led her in; and the cover of the basket came off, so that the meats in it fell all about. Then everybody laughed and jeered at her; and she was so abashed that she wished herself a thousand feet deep in the earth. She sprang to the door to run away; but on the steps King Grisly-Beard overtook and brought her back, and said, "Fear me not! I am the musician who has lived with you in the hut: I brought you there because I loved you. I am also the soldier who overset your stall. I have done all this only to cure you of pride, and to punish you for the ill-treatment you bestowed on me.

"Now all is over; you have learnt wisdom, your faults are gone, and it is time to celebrate our marriage feast!"

Then the chamberlains came and brought her the most beautiful robes: and her father and his whole court were there already, and congratulated her on her marriage. Joy was in every face. The feast was grand, and all were merry; and I wish you and I had been of the party.